Carlos & Carmen

The Costume Contest

by Kirsten McDonald
illustrated by Erika Meza

Calico Kid

An Imprint of Magic Wagon
abdopublishing.com

*For the StoryWeavers who always said
that Carlos and Carmen were winners —KKM*

*For my two little brothers, Pedro y Gustavo, who would let me dress
them up and come up with ridiculous costume antics. —EM*

abdopublishing.com

Published by Magic Wagon, a division of ABDO, PO Box 398166, Minneapolis, Minnesota 55439. Copyright © 2017 by Abdo Consulting Group, Inc. International copyrights reserved in all countries. No part of this book may be reproduced in any form without written permission from the publisher. Calico Kid™ is a trademark and logo of Magic Wagon.

Printed in the United States of America, North Mankato, Minnesota.
102016
012017

Written by Kirsten McDonald
Illustrated by Erika Meza
Edited by Heidi M.D. Elston
Design Contributors: Christina Doffing & Candice Keimig

Publisher's Cataloging in Publication Data

Names: McDonald, Kirsten, author. | Meza, Erika, illustrator.
Title: The costume contest / by Kirsten McDonald ; illustrated by Erika Meza.
Description: Minneapolis, MN : Magic Wagon, 2017. | Series: Carlos & Carmen
Summary: Fall leaves and pumpkins everywhere. Carlos and Carmen are making plans to be in a costume contest, but neither of them wants the other to lose. It's a problem. A prize winning problem! But with an old shirt, a pair of scissors, and a lot of creativity, the twins come up with a prize winning solution.
Identifiers: LCCN 2016947496 | ISBN 9781624021824 (lib. bdg.) |
ISBN 9781624022425 (ebook) | ISBN 9781624022722 (Read-to-me ebook)
Subjects: LCSH: Hispanic American families—Juvenile fiction. | Twins—Juvenile fiction. | Brothers and sisters—Juvenile fiction. | Costume—Juvenile fiction. | Contests—Juvenile fiction.
Classification: DDC [E]—dc23
LC record available at http://lccn.loc.gov/2016947496

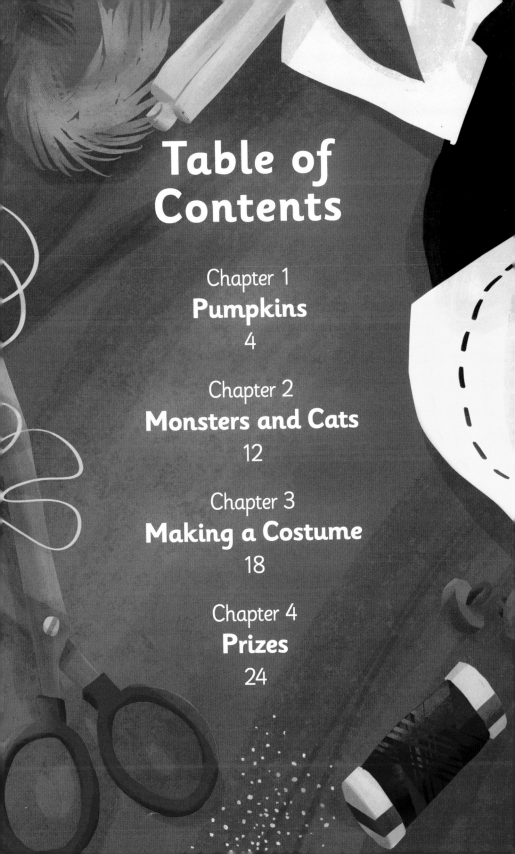

Table of Contents

Chapter 1
Pumpkins

It was fall, and pumpkins were popping up everywhere. There were pumpkins in the stores. There were pumpkins in the schools.

And, there was a big pumpkin in the Garcias' kitchen.

Papá spread out newspaper. "This will make it easy to clean up," he said.

"We won't make a mess," said Carmen.

"We're expert calabaza carvers," added Carlos.

Mamá spread out more paper. "You can't be too prepared," she said.

"Our calabaza should be a happy jack-o'-lantern," said Carlos.

"With a big sonrisa," said Carmen.

"And teeth poking out of its smile," added Carlos.

"And a tongue poking out of the sonrisa, too," said Carmen.

"Not so fast, mis hijos," said Papá. "First, you have to hollow out the pumpkin."

Carmen reached into the pumpkin. She pulled out a handful of slippery seeds. She tossed them on the paper.

Carlos reached into the pumpkin. He pulled out a handful of squishy strings. He plopped them on the paper.

Spooky poked the slippery seeds. She batted the squishy strings. She skittered all around the pumpkin.

Soon Spooky had seeds and strings
scattered everywhere. She even had a
pumpkin seed stuck to her nose.

"¡Ya basta!" said Mamá, scooping
up Spooky. "It's time for you to go
outside."

Spooky swished her tail. Poking seeds was fun. But pouncing on fallen leaves was even better.

Chapter 2
Monsters and Cats

When the Garcias were finished,
they had a very happy jack-o'-lantern.
It had big, circle eyes and a triangle
nose.

It had a poking-out tongue and jaggedy teeth. And, it had a smile so big it looked like it was laughing.

Papá said, "Guess what, mis hijos?"

"What?" asked Carlos and Carmen.

"There's a costume contest at the park next weekend," said Papá.

"Hooray!" said Carlos. "Let's be in the disfraz contest."

"Double hooray!" said Carmen.
"Let's win a prize!"

"I'll be a monstruo," Carlos said.

"I'll be a gata," said Carmen.

"I want to have the best costume," said Carlos. "I want to win a premio."

"Yo también!" said Carmen, imagining the prize.

Then Carlos looked at Carmen.
Carmen looked at Carlos. The double-
hooray crashed in to no hooray at all.

"But, if I win the prize," said
Carlos, "then you won't."

"And, if I win the prize," said
Carmen, "then you won't."

It was a problem. A prize-winning
problem.

All of a sudden, Carmen's eyes got really big and sparkly.

At the same time, Carlos's smile got really big and toothy.

"Are you thinking what I'm thinking?" they asked each other.

And because they were twins, they were.

Chapter 3
Making a Costume

Carlos and Carmen told their

parents all about their idea.

"I can help," said Mamá.

"Yo también," said Papá.

Carlos got scissors and markers.

Carmen got cloth and stuffing.

Papá got an old T-shirt.

Mamá got the sewing machine.

Then they all got busy.

Carlos and Carmen took turns cutting the cloth. Then Mamá sewed it into part of the costume.

Papá gave the twins his big, old shirt. Carlos drew on one half of the shirt. Carmen drew on the other half.

"Do you think we'll win a premio?" Carlos asked.

"Maybe," said Carmen. "So far, our disfraz is a little bit cute."

"And, a little bit scary," said Carlos.

Carlos and Carmen cut some more cloth.

Mamá sewed some more seams.

And, Papá stuffed fluff into some parts of the costume.

Carlos held up the shirt. "It's looking really good," he said.

Carmen held up the part Mamá had sewn. "We're sure to win a premio," she said.

Mamá and Papá looked at the costume. They looked at the twins and laughed.

Papá said, "No one else will have a costume like yours."

"That's for sure," said Mamá.

23

Chapter 4
Prizes

On Saturday, the Garcia family went to the park. They saw princesses and pirates. They saw robots and rabbits. They saw a family of crayons.

"There are a lot of good costumes here," said Carlos.

"Yes," said Carmen, "but our disfraz is superduper special."

"That's one way to describe it, Carmencita," said Papá with a wink.

Carlos and Carmen walked to the costume judging area. The judges walked all around the people in costumes.

"Do you really think we'll win a premio?" Carlos asked Carmen.

Carmen said, "We have a tail, and we are cute. I think we will win a prize."

"We also have horns, and we are scary," said Carlos. "So, maybe you are right."

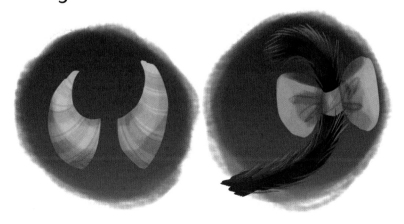

Carmen swished her tail and meowed.

Carlos waved his monster claws and growled.

"What exactly are you?" asked one of the judges.

"We're a two-headed cat monster!" the twins said.

The judge scrunched up her eyebrows. She started to laugh.

"This is definitely the most original costume!" the judge said. She pulled out a fancy prize ribbon. She pinned it to Papá's biggest, oldest shirt.

"Hooray!" shouted Carlos and Carmen. "We won a premio!"

"And we both got to win," said Carlos.

"And we both got to be what we wanted," said Carmen.

Mamá and Papá admired the fancy prize ribbon. And, they hugged the two-headed cat monster.

Then the Garcias held hands as they headed toward home and more fall fun.

Spanish to English

calabaza – pumpkin

disfraz – costume

gata – girl cat

Mamá – Mommy

mis hijos – my children

monstruo – monster

Papá – Daddy

premio – prize

sonrisa – smile

¡Ya basta! – That's enough!

yo también – me too